The Hidden Triceratops

by Richard Bevan

illustrated by Io Shepard

ChangeStart
PRESS

For Gaelen and Nick

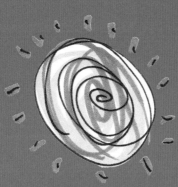

Publisher's Cataloging-in-Publication Data
Richard Bevan (author)
and Io Shepard (illustrator)
Design by Bill Greaves, Concept West

The Hidden Triceratops
ISBN-13: 978-0-9835588-9-7
Library of Congress Control Number: 2020945099
Juvenile Fiction > Animals > Dinosaurs & Prehistoric Creatures

For information contact ChangeStart Press, Seattle, WA
www.changestart.com

An apologetic note to zoologists and paleontologists: the author realizes that, strictly speaking, Pteranodons are pterosaurs and not dinosaurs. But pterosaurs and dinosaurs do both fall within the clade avemetatarsalia. So I hope you don't mind that I have followed popular usage that interprets 'dinosaur' as broadly describing all the creatures of the Cretaceous era.

CHAPTER ONE

The Ancient Jungle

Let's imagine a very dense and ancient jungle. It's green, lush and steamy. There are many strange and wonderful smells. In some places it's dark even in daytime because the trees are so thick. There is heavy undergrowth: bushes, tangled roots, mushrooms, flowers and some dangling vines. There are also huge fallen trees, some boulders and rocky outcrops.

If you listen you can hear many different sounds. Some of these might seem familiar, like running water in a stream, or the wind stirring the leaves on the trees.

But others sound a little **strange**. There are some snuffling noises; some grunts; some squeaks and chirps. There may even be an occasional **ROAR** or **growl**.

And there are perhaps some heavy THUMPS and crashing noises. They sound as if something LARGE is moving through the jungle.

What do you think might be making those sounds? Birds? People? Animals? Did someone say **dinosaurs**? I think you might have peeked ahead, but you are correct. The **Ancient Steamy Jungle** is home to many dinosaurs.

That's because the story is happening a very, very, very, long time ago. Tens of millions of years ago, actually, **and before there were even any people!**

How could there not be any people? Well, that's **another** story. For now, we just need to know that dinosaurs make most of those sounds. And there are many different sounds, because there are many different dinosaurs. They come in ALL shapes and sizes, as we'll see later. And some—including one of our characters—can fly.

But before we hear more about them, there's a bit more imagining to do. We are at the **edge** of the jungle (luckily not on the middle where we could very easily get lost). Here, there aren't nearly as many trees and the undergrowth is much less dense. In front of us is a **Wide Grassy Plain.**

In the far, far, far distance a range of huge mountains rises up to snowcapped peaks. One of them is especially high, its summit often hidden in cloud and mist. This is the **Distant Misty Mountain.** And actually it's a **volcano**, which means that occasionally it erupts with fire and lava and smoke. But luckily it's a LONG way away.

Much nearer than the mountain is the **Great Blue Lake**, round which groups of creatures of all sizes gather. Some of them are drinking. A few are swimming or floating, perhaps to cool down. A few more are wading and occasionally ducking down to grab a fish or a crab. And others are just resting or relaxing.

CHAPTER TWO

All Shapes and Sizes

Food is very important for all the dinosaurs. They spend a lot of time looking for food, eating it, and then sleeping to digest it.

Luckily, many of the plants in the jungle are good to eat. There are mushrooms, roots, ferns, and all kinds of leaves. And there are also many different trees and shrubs with delicious fruit and berries. Food can be found out in the Wide Grassy Plain as well, including (of course) plenty of grass!

Many of the dinosaurs spend time out on the plain as well as in the jungle. The lake is a good place to catch fish, and also to cool down when it's hot. And of course there is plenty of water to drink. Getting around on the plain is certainly a lot easier than pushing through the dense and steamy jungle.

Many dinosaurs are mild and friendly. And although there are others that can be **rather fierce**, even those seem to be peaceful when they're at the lake. It's important to them all, partly because it is of course the easiest place to find water. Those gathered around are all shapes and sizes. And everyone seems to get along fine.

But **away** from the lake the smaller creatures need to keep away from the larger and fiercer (and hungrier) ones. I'm afraid to say that some of those larger dinosaurs see the smaller ones (including those in our story) as **food**.

But if you think that is scary, now is a good time to remember this: even if parts of the story might be slightly scary, it is just a **story**. There is a VERY GOOD CHANCE that it will have a happy ending.

Some of those young dinosaurs will grow up to be large, strong and able to defend themselves. But when they are younger and smaller they have to be fast and **smart**. They need to be able to stay away (or get away) from hungry larger dinosaurs.

Rex

CHAPTER THREE

The Dinosaurs in the Story

Let's talk about our main characters. At this time (as I said, a **very** long time ago) the earth is occupied by all kinds of different dinosaurs. Some are very small: about the size of a chicken. Others are very large indeed, even AS BIG AS A SCHOOL BUS! Can you imagine a creature that size (bigger than an elephant)? And some of the flying dinosaurs were as big as a small plane.

We should know about one special character, the fiercest of all dinosaurs. He isn't the BIGGEST of all but he is certainly very large and extremely strong. And he is often hungry! He is a Tyrannosaurus Rex, or T. Rex for short. He is known throughout the Ancient Steamy Jungle as the **Great Dinosaur of the North**. And he is also known as **Very Fierce And Not To Be Messed With!**

But though the T. Rex is large and ferocious, all the young dinosaurs refer to him simply as Rex. It makes him seem slightly less scary. The young dinosaurs dream about finding ways to evade and outwit him. And as it happens, although certainly large, strong and fierce, Rex is perhaps not the **smartest** of the various dinosaurs. The smaller ones can sometimes trick him.

SKi

So now it's time to meet the two dinosaurs that this story is mostly about. (And if someone said, "About time too" I quite understand.) One is a young **Triceratops** called José. The other is a young **Pteranodon** called Ski.

José

CHAPTER FOUR

The young Triceratops

José the young Triceratops is about two feet long (at the time of the story) and a foot high. His family lives near the edge of the jungle in a large cave in a rocky outcrop. But they like to go out to the plain where there is plenty of grass, and many other kinds of plants as well.

José already has three small horns, one at the front of his head and two on the sides. These will grow much bigger. They will be very useful if he needs to defend himself against an attack by one of the fiercer dinosaurs. He also has a sort of bony collar above and round his neck that helps to protect him. It's rather like armor. And it can actually change color, for example if he's excited or angry.

When the story starts José is looking out of the cave and thinking about heading out for a walk to find some food.

Like all Triceratops he spends a lot of time exploring for food and grazing. He eats moss, grass, mushrooms and sometimes flowers and tree bark. But his most regular meals—because there are plenty of them—are palm leaves and ferns. And he certainly likes a few berries if he can find them.

Palm leaves are very tough and need a great deal of chewing, but as it happens the Triceratops have LOTS of teeth—hundreds of them! So chewing isn't a problem.

What do you think about that diet? Maybe we should eat bark, roots, and ferns? No? Maybe just the berries!

In the last few months José has been finding his own way around and has come across some excellent berry patches. These are in places that the larger dinosaurs can't reach because of tree roots and branches. José is small enough to find his way through these. Sometimes he has to crouch down and hide when a large dinosaur is passing.

On this morning he set out on his own, leaving the rest of the family asleep. He was thinking about a good breakfast of roots and mushrooms, perhaps with a bit of bark to provide something crunchy.

He had already decided to go slightly further than usual. Perhaps he could even find some **early-ripening berries** as dessert. Occasionally he stopped to listen (and look up) in case any **dangerous larger jungle residents** were nearby.

José had a good drink at a stream and chewed some tasty (although rather tough) palm fronds. He crossed the stream at a shallow place and walked on. He pushed his way through the tangled undergrowth, snacking as he went. After a while he was in an area where he hadn't been before. Tramping through the jungle can be hard work. José was a bit tired, and rather sleepy.

We'll come back to see how José does soon, but first we'll meet the other young dinosaur.

18

CHAPTER FIVE

The young Pteranodon

Ski the young Pteranodon has long narrow wings that are about three feet wide when fully extended. She has short legs and sharp claws. She uses these for grabbing onto branches—or perhaps for holding a fish or small creature that she has caught.

She is already good at flying and often takes off to go exploring on her own. She can walk around on the ground, and even run if she has to (though not very fast). That will become important later in the story!

Her family live in a very large nest half way up a rocky cliff. Two huge trees grow up from near the base. The Pteranodons can easily cross between the nest and the upper branches of the trees.

They do this to get to a good perch for a lookout, or to get ready to fly down to the forest floor. They like to visit some of the streams and ponds where they can find fish.

From their nest the Pteranodon family can see across the tops of the trees to the edge of the Wide Grassy Plain. And although the family likes to have their nest hidden away in the jungle, they often spend the daylight hours in the open. They fly above the tops of the trees, occasionally finding their way through the branches and landing for food or a rest. Or they soar out over the plain.

When she was younger and smaller Ski ate mainly insects, and also fish that her parents brought to her. But now she can catch her own fish with her long beak or with her claws. She can easily swoop down on a river or lake and make a catch. And she can also catch some smaller creatures rather like mice. So that's her main diet, together with some crab and also occasionally berries.

Between them the two young dinosaurs can eat pretty much any food they can find. (Which would **you** prefer: Ski's diet of fish and very small animals, or José's diet of plants?)

Ski's little brother Firi was still learning to fly. The whole family was busy hauling him up to a high branch with a clear space below.

Then they would push him off (or he jumped, once he knew they'd catch him if it didn't quite work). They circled round as he learned to glide or struggled to flap his small wings, tweeting anxiously as he did so. They showed Firi how to do this and helped him land. Although he could now stop his fall he still needed to practice turning. But it certainly sounds like FUN, doesn't it?

Firi was beginning to catch on, and was starting to enjoy it. But the practice seemed likely to go on for a while. So Ski decided to go exploring.

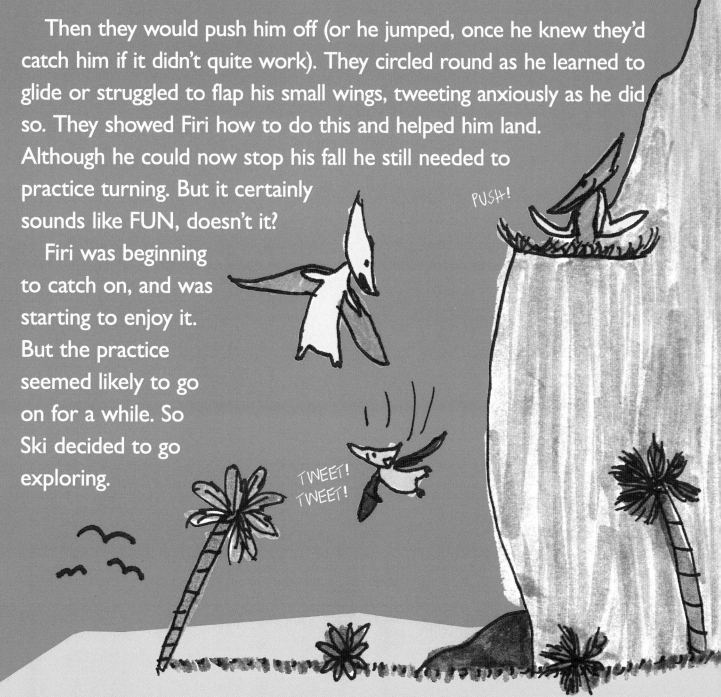

PUSH!

TWEET! TWEET!

CHAPTER SIX

José and Ski Meet

Meanwhile, José was looking for a place to take a nap. The jungle here was less dense. Plenty of sky could be seen. A steep cliff rose up at one side and on the other side José could just see the plain. Two tall trees grew up from the base of the cliff, where there were some large boulders.

The sun rose, and José, who by now had eaten enough **breakfast** to more than make up for missing **dinner**, began to feel even more sleepy. So he found a shady and hidden spot among the boulders.

These boulders had a greenish color rather like José's tough hide. He thought they would help to make him hard to spot **should any unfriendly creatures be around**. He settled down in the middle of them and dragged some branches and leaves up around him. That made him even less visible to any large and hungry dinosaur that might be nearby. He could hear some sounds and flapping from far above, but didn't worry about them and soon dropped off to sleep.

(Any ideas about the sounds and the flapping? What or who might be making that noise?)

Just at this time Ski was ready to set out exploring. And although it was easier to stay high up, away from the branches and vines, she had decided to look for a new fishing spot in a pond or stream.

So she glided around and down, staying close to the cliff and out of the way of the flying lesson. She spotted a rounded gray-green boulder by the base of one of the trees. It was a nice shady spot.

The boulder had what looked like three sticks at one end. The sticks didn't have any leaves but Ski thought they were growing just beyond the boulder.

So she swooped down and made a neat landing. Her talons found an easy grip. The boulder didn't seem as hard or rocky as she'd expected but it was a comfortable perch.

After a moment to settle, Ski folded her wings.

Then the boulder moved! The rather surprised Ski saw that what she had thought were branches were actually the horns of a young Triceratops. It was of course José, who had lifted and turned his head, and was now looking up at Ski. He was just as surprised as she was.

The two young dinosaurs looked at each other for a moment. Then they spoke at the same time.

"Sorry, but I'm not actually a landing spot," said José.

And Ski said, "I'm sorry too, I thought you were a nice rocky perch."

Ski flapped her wings and flew up and onto a leaning tree just above them. José stretched then relaxed again, still in among the rocks. They looked at each other, and each saw that the other was friendly. Then José said, "I was just having a nap. But if you're interested, I found a good place to get berries."

CHAPTER SEVEN

Time to Explore

"I was going to look for something to eat as well," said Ski. Perhaps even some fish. Do you like fish?"

"I don't," said José. "We mostly eat plants. But I do know a nice stream with a pool that I often drink from. And I've seen fish in it. Would you like to take a look?"

"I certainly would," replied Ski. "Let's see what we can find."

José hiked and Ski flew, and they soon reached the pool. Ski was able to glide down and land on the small beach.

She stood at the edge with her wings out, watching carefully. Suddenly she darted forward, flew a short way and hit the water with a SPLOOSH—claws first. She flapped back into the air clasping a fish. Then she tossed it up and as it turned she caught it and swallowed.

If José could clap he would have done so. "Very good," he said. "I knew this would be a good spot for you. See if you can get another."

For a while the young dinosaurs continued to look for food. And if it seems as if this is what they spend much of their time doing, that's probably right. It takes a lot of time to chew and digest raw food. (We're very lucky that we can cook. This makes everything much easier to eat.)

After a while they decided to explore a little further. The jungle was dense, but José could knock branches and other obstacles out of the way with his three horns and his thick hide. But Ski could hardly get anywhere on the ground with her long wings, unless there was some open space. So she flapped her way up through the branches of a big tree until she was high enough to launch into flight.

José pushed briskly along. Ski flew above and kept him in sight.

They met up again in a clearing. José was in a patch of berries having a fine time. Ski glided down and perched on a low branch. She was looking intently at the ground.

"What are you looking at?" asked José.

"Take a look," replied Ski.

It was a HUGE claw-print with what looked like three very large talons. It was about the same length as José. The print looked freshly made.

The young dinosaurs looked at it for a few moments.

Then Ski said, "There's only one creature in the jungle that could have left these."

"Yikes! I'm afraid you're right," replied José. "And just when I was ready for another nap. It's certainly Rex. He must be nearby. Sometimes I wish I could fly!"

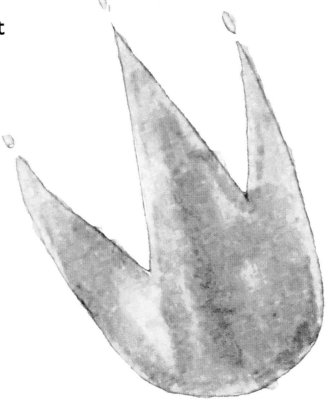

CHAPTER EIGHT

Here Comes Rex

"Yes. It's Rex all right," said Ski. "Only the Great Dinosaur of the North could have made those prints."

"We haven't heard him for a while," said José, "but the prints are really fresh. He must be nearby, although I can't hear anything. Usually he's pretty noisy."

"Maybe he's taking a nap?" suggested Ski. "If he shows up I'll be fine, I can take to the air. But you need to be ready to hide."

"My parents tell me to find a small cave or space in tree roots—somewhere that I can fit but he's too big to reach in," replied José. "I think I'm going to take a look around: maybe my berry patch will work; that's really hard for any large creature to get into."

At that moment they heard a distant BOOM and several THUMPS

and a ROAR, followed by a sound like a strong wind. There was no doubt that Rex was coming in their direction.

"Quick, get into your hiding place," said Ski. José turned, and ran back down the trail they'd made. He quickly found his safe hiding place among the twisted roots of a two old leaning trees. He wriggled down among the berries that grew there. His hide was thick enough not to be hurt by the thorns. He peeked out through a gap between the roots. He hoped that even if the Great Dinosaur saw him he would still be safe. But Rex was very big and very strong, so José was certainly a bit worried.

Ski hopped onto a nearby branch, ready to take to the air at any moment.

The sounds of the approaching dinosaur became louder and closer. Suddenly Rex burst into the clearing. His huge head was swaying from side to side as if he were looking for something—or someone. And José realized too late that leading directly from the main trail was a smaller trail that he'd made just by tramping through the long grass. The trail, which Rex had just noticed, led directly to José's hiding place!

The Chase

Rex gave another **ROAR** and started along the well-marked path. Of course, the huge dinosaur trampled everything. He turned what had been a little path into a much larger one. José squeezed back and made himself as small and hard to see as he could. He **hoped** he couldn't be spotted through the roots that formed a sort of protective cage. But he certainly didn't **know** that they would keep him safe.

The giant Tyrannosaur stopped and started to bend down his huge head to look at what the trail led to. But suddenly a small creature with folded wings ran across the path right in front of Rex. It was Ski, squawking as she ran just a few feet away. And yes, she wasn't flying: she was **running**. This was an activity that she wasn't very good at with her long wings rather in the way.

The sight of a small Pteranodon running across his path certainly got Rex's attention. He turned away from José's safe place, gave a growl and took a mighty swipe with one of his short arms. By then Ski had scuttled past Rex and was heading back the way she had come. She didn't run especially well, but nor did Rex until he got up to full speed. And he needed a lot of open space to do that.

José knew that Ski was staying on the ground so Rex would keep chasing her. He might give up if Ski took to the air.

THUD

Ski kept going on the path and back to the main trail, turning away from the stream. Rex followed, roaring. Just as it seemed he was going to grab Ski, the young Pteranadon made a great leap, pushing off with her folded wings. She opened them and rose gracefully into the air. Rex roared again, reached up, stretched out—and tripped over a fallen tree. The **THUD** as he hit the ground echoed through the forest. Many hidden creatures squeaked or chirped or roared.

CHAPTER TEN

José and Ski Reunite

Rex slowly rose to his feet, shaking his head, and looking in the direction that Ski had flown. She was circling above, fully in Rex's view and not far away—but clearly out of reach. Rex dropped his great head and set off along the trail towards his lair. He knew he couldn't catch Ski and had forgotten about his investigation of the small path—and José.

José had seen and heard it all. Once Rex was out of sight, and the jungle had settled down again, he wriggled out of his hiding place and went back to the clearing. Ski glided back, made a neat landing, and rejoined him, saying, "I think I'm better at flying than running!"

"You were running pretty well," said José. "That was brilliant. Thanks so very much. I do hope that I can do the same for you one day. Although I'm not sure how I could do it without flying."

"Don't mention it," replied Ski. "It was fun. I'll do it any time we need to. But I won't take so long to get airborne next time!"

"Rex certainly had quite a fall," said José, and Ski replied, "Yes, I almost felt sorry for him when I heard the crash."

"But it was just as well he did trip," replied José. He thought about this for a moment, and then added, "So what shall we do now?"

Ski had the answer. "Perhaps we should be friends and do more exploring and even have some more adventures?"

"Sounds good to me!" replied José. "As long as we don't run into the Great Dinosaur of the North again."

"Don't worry about Rex," sad Ski. We can hear him coming from miles away and I can fly and you can hide. He'll never catch us. After all, we got away from him today, didn't we? We can do it every time!"

And let's certainly hope that she's correct!

Made in the USA
Columbia, SC
28 January 2021